Honey's Hive

Mo O'Hara

ILLUSTRATED BY

Aya Kakeda

ANDERSEN PRESS

HONEY

BELLA

BEANIE

FRED

BOB

HEX

NANA

MISS IVY

THE QUEEN

Chapter 1

The sun was beginning to warm the air in the little garden by the cottage. Honey buzzed around the flowerpots next to the hive, her stripy fuzz all blown about and her wonky antennae twitching with excitement.

'Major Honey to Ground Control. It looks like a rocky entry, but don't worry, danger is my middle name,' Honey shouted into an imaginary walkie talkie. 'Over and out.'

I should explain. Honey's middle name was not actually 'Danger.' She didn't even have a middle name. Most bees don't. And she was not in any real danger either. There isn't much danger you can get into when you're flying around two feet off the ground.

But Honey liked to be a little . . . well . . . dramatic.

She was supposed to be practising her flower landings for Bee School, but Honey was putting it off. *Procrastinating*. And she knew exactly what that word meant because someone was always telling Honey that she was procrastinating. Pretty much every day.

Sometimes, when Honey was supposed to be studying hive history, really she would be imagining herself as the queen of an ancient Egyptian beehive.

Sometimes, when she was supposed to be learning an important waggle dance, really she would be imagining that she was twirling pirouettes like a swooping swarm of swallows.

Today she was supposed to be practising how to land on a flower head to collect pollen (a fairly essential life skill for a bee) but instead she was picturing herself as the first bee to land on the moon.

'Shhhiss.' Honey made her voice sound like an astronaut speaking through a space helmet. 'One small step for a bee. One giant leap for bee-kind.'

She stepped onto a geranium. In her head she seemed to glide onto the surface of the moon. In reality, she overbalanced and the flower tipped, sending Honey tumbling antenna-first into the dirt.

'Ooooof! Hmmm . . . More like a crash landing,' she mumbled as she shook the dirt off her stripy fuzz.

A ladybird fluttered down and landed on the rim of the flowerpot.

'You're an early bird this morning,' Nana Ladybird said.

'You know what they say . . . the early bird catches the worm,' Honey replied.

A brown wrinkly worm reared his head up from a mound of dirt in the pot.

'Bird?! Where?!' he shouted. 'Where's the bird?'

'Oh, there's no bird! It's just a saying,' Honey said.

The worm slumped back on the ground. 'Phew,' he said. 'It's a very upsetting saying.'

'Sorry,' Honey replied as the worm disappeared back into the dirt.

'Hey, Nana Ladybird,' Honey said, 'what's the buzz? Anything interesting happened since yesterday?'

'The ants had about a hundred new kids,' Nana answered.

'Congrats!' Honey hollered over to a very tired-looking ant walking up her anthill.

'And Bob the caterpillar has nearly finished his cocoon.'

'Looking good,' Honey called to Bob.

The caterpillar beamed awkwardly and waved several of his legs.

'And no sign of that spaceman breaking into your hive,' Nana said.

'Nana, I've told you, he's not a spaceman. He just wears that big outfit with the head cover because he thinks it protects him from getting stung,' Honey said. Then she leaned into Nana and whispered, 'But we could totally sting him if we wanted to.'

'He's a spaceman!' Nana insisted.

'He's a hu-man,' Honey said. 'He calls himself a "beekeeper" which is totally lame. Like he keeps *us*? *We* keep *him*. We share our honey with him. We should call ourselves human keepers.'

Nana laughed. 'Anyway, aren't you supposed to be in Bee School, Honey?' she asked.

'No, it's OK, I don't have any lessons today. I have my worker bee meeting with the headteacher later.'

'Worker bee meeting?'

'Yes. Every young bee has to have a talk

with her to decide their bee job for when they grow up. Today is a taster day where I can try out the worker bee jobs and see what suits me.' Then Honey stopped and looked up at the sun. 'Oh no! I'm late! I'd better shake a wing! My best friends Hex and Beanie have already had their meetings, I can't be late for mine. Miss Ivy will make me recite the Bee Code a hundred times in detention.' She paused. 'Again.'

'What's the Bee Code?' Nana asked.

Honey clasped two of her arms in front of her and saluted with another one.

'A bee must . . .

Bee loyal, bee strong.

You must always get along.

Bee considerate, bee kind.

Work hard and you'll find

Your place in the hive.

You'll help it survive.

Together, you see,

You can be your best bee.'

'Sounds like you know it well, dear,' Nana smiled.

'When you have to recite something a hundred times it kinda sticks in your head,' Honey nodded. 'It's just so Bee-centric. You know what I mean, Nana?'

'Not really, dear, you *are* a bee.'

'But being a bee is soooooo booooooring. Humans and other animals have a much better time. Birds get to migrate and travel to exotic places. Squirrels get to do all kinds of cool acrobatics to find food and hide nuts. And caterpillars get to transform into totally different insects altogether.'

'Yeah, I'm a bit nervous about all that transforming stuff actually,' Bob the caterpillar shouted over.

'You got this, Bob. I'm totally jealous,' Honey hollered back. 'You'll make a fab butterfly. Anyway, what was I saying?' she said to Nana.

'How boring it is to be a bee.'

'Yeah, and humans get to have all kinds of adventures like skateboarding and rowing boats and landing on the moon – and what do we get to do? Buzz around.'

'You get to pollinate plants and make honey,' Nana smiled. 'And be a part of your hive. *That's* important.'

'But it's not EXCITING, Nana.'

'You young insects and your excitement. In my day we were grateful for an occasional aphid for a treat.'

I should let you know that at this point a tiny, tiny aphid who was crawling along the leaf nearby quickly turned around and headed back the other way muttering, 'Why does everyone want to eat me? Why can't we all just get along?' in a tiny, tiny aphid voice. Unfortunately, he turned around right into the path of a very hungry beetle. Ah, the circle of life – but that's another story.

'Anyway, gotta go. Bye, Nana Ladybird!'

Honey made a beeline (see what I did there?) for the hive.

She zoomed into the entrance, rounded the corner, and slammed straight into her big sister Bella who was guarding the way.

'Aaaaah!'

Chapter 2

Honey barrelled into Bella, and they tumbled across the floor in a sprawl of flailing antennae, arms and legs. They landed in a jumbled heap against a wax wall.

Bella jumped up and shook herself off. This was clearly not the first time she had been barrelled into by her little sister. Bella was a whole head taller than Honey and broader across the shoulders. She was always neat and disciplined and aside from them having the same zigzag on their heads you would never suspect they were sisters – even though everyone in the hive was actually related. The Queen bee was everyone's mum. (It's a bee thing. We'll get to that later.)

'Hey, not so fast, Honey,' Bella said and she scooped up Honey and plonked her back on her feet.

'But I'm late . . .' Honey stammered.

'I know,' Bella replied. 'For your meeting with Miss Ivy. 'Look at you though.' Bella ushered Honey outside and rolled her eyes. 'You have to make a good impression, Honey. Come on . . . straighten your antennae.' She adjusted Honey's antennae so they weren't pointing out in opposite directions, but they immediately flopped down again. 'And brush off your fuzz. You look like you've been rolling in dirt or something.' Bella quickly dusted off Honey's stripes with four of her arms at once.

'OK?' Honey asked.

'Yeah, you'll be fine. Just be polite, stand up straight and look her right in her composite eyes and tell her what you want to do as a worker bee.'

'There's only one problem with that,' Honey said. 'I have NO IDEA what I want to do!'

'Then SHE'LL tell YOU what you're going to do,' Bella said.

'But what if . . .' Honey started.

'Come on, you can do this. You're not a little larva any more. Off you go. Good luck,' Bella said and patted Honey on the back. 'Right. It's down this hall, then left, then up, then through the tunnel and up one more level. Five honeycombs up, second cell to the left . . .'

'Right.' Honey nodded.

'No, left.' Bella shook her antennae. 'Oh. Just go.'

Honey zoomed off to the honeycomb cell where Miss Ivy was waiting for the interview.

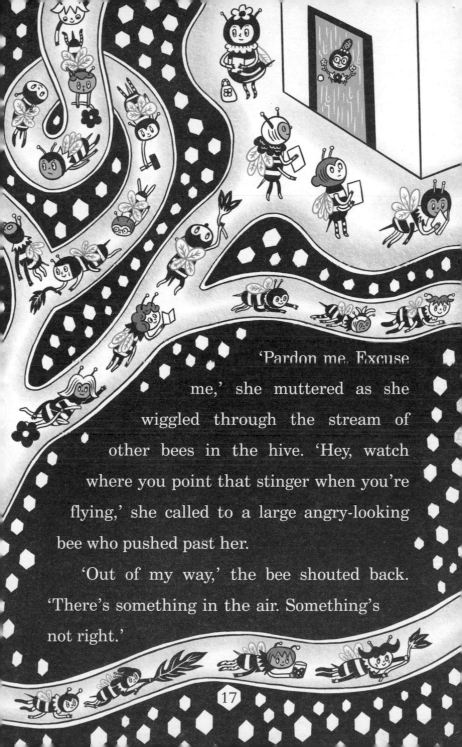

'Pardon me. Excuse me,' she muttered as she wiggled through the stream of other bees in the hive. 'Hey, watch where you point that stinger when you're flying,' she called to a large angry-looking bee who pushed past her.

'Out of my way,' the bee shouted back. 'There's something in the air. Something's not right.'

Just to let you know - this is one of those moments in books where there is a hint that something is going to happen. It's not a subtle thing that we storytellers do but it's useful and, on this occasion, it is totally correct so I might as well not hint but just come right out and tell you that something is *definitely* going to happen. (And to be honest you were expecting that anyway because nobody actually picks up a book where they hope nothing happens.) Anyway, we'll leave the fortune-telling gloomy bee for the moment and get back to Honey, who is still blissfully unaware of the events that are about to unfold.

'Wow, who stubbed her stinger this morning?' Honey mumbled to herself as she rounded the corner to Miss Ivy's cell.

When she got there, she tentatively tapped on the door. 'May I come in?'

Miss Ivy called from inside. 'Due to being

late, please recite the
Bee Code. Ten times
before entering.'

'Not again,'
Honey mumbled.
Then in a louder
voice she began,
'A bee must . . .'

I think we can skip this bit as you have already
heard the Bee Code (important as it is). But there
are a few other facts you should know about life in a
beehive before we go on.

So, for those of you who haven't been in a hive
before I'll buzz though the basics.

1. There are a lot of bees. Really a lot of bees. More
    bees than you can imagine could fit into a wooden
    box like this. I mean think of a number of bees
    and then double that and then double that and

then times it by a hundred. Between twenty and eighty THOUSAND bees can live in a single hive. Honey's hive has about twenty thousand bees. (If they were people, they would fill a stadium.)

2. Everybody is always busy. You know that phrase 'busy as a bee'. Totally 100 percent accurate.

3. The bees build a honeycomb to live in, raise larvae, make wax, gather pollen, nectar and water, and make honey. They also look after the queen.

4. There is one queen in a hive. She is the mother of all the bees in that hive. Then about ten per cent of the other bees are drones. They are the male bees who make baby bees with the Queen. Then the other ninety per cent of the population are female worker bees. The worker bees do ALL the jobs in the hive so that the queen and drones can make more bees. Got it? Sometimes another queen emerges but we'll get to that in due course.

5.   The hive works as well as it does because everyone just gets on and does their job.

Sometimes, very rarely, a bee comes along who is a bit out of step with the whole 'you get a job and you do it' vibe of the hive. So, say if, for instance, a bee wants to go out and have adventures instead of taking on a regular worker job then this might be a bit of a problem for a headteacher bee to deal with.

And that brings us nicely back to Honey and where we left off.

Chapter 3

Honey droned on, '. . . *You can be your best bee.*'
She paused and then called through the door. 'Is
that ten times?'

'Close enough. I lost count,' Miss Ivy said.
'Come in.'

Honey fluttered through the entrance. Miss
Ivy's office had glossy wax walls with images of
important past bees etched onto them. Builder
bees, guard bees, forager bees, and of course
the Queen bee herself. Honey was literally
surrounded by important bees with important
bee jobs. I'm not going to lie, she found it a little
intimidating.

'So, Honey, we are at the stage in our bee

life where we think about the future role we will undertake to contribute to the welfare of the hive.'

Miss Ivy sometimes did that thing where she referred to a student as 'we'. Probably because the whole culture of being a bee is about working as a team, being 'we' rather than 'you' or 'me'. Or maybe it's just that Miss Ivy liked to confuse the students sitting opposite her. If that was the case, then she was certainly succeeding now.

'WE are at the stage in OUR bee life?' Honey said. 'Sorry did I miss something? Oh, are you looking for a new job too, Miss Ivy?'

'We are perfectly happy with our career,' Miss Ivy said.

'And we are perfectly happy being a bee student for now so maybe we can put this whole thing off for another season or two and come back to it when I know what I want to do.' Honey started to stand up.

'Sit,' Miss Ivy ordered.

Honey sat.

'What worker bee job are we . . .' she paused, 'are *you* thinking of, Honey?'

'I suppose the main role of queen is already taken for a while, huh?'

'Yes.'

'Then what about a bee adventurer? Or bee reporter? Oh . . . or a bee astronaut would be fantastic,' Honey said.

Miss Ivy sighed and pointed to a list of jobs etched onto one of the walls:

'We could be a larvae nurse and look after all the little larvae when they are hatched.

'We could be a cleaner bee and tidy up the hive and clean the cells.

'We could be
a helper for the
Queen, and groom
her and get her food.

'We could be a
builder bee and
construct the cells
in the honeycomb.

'We could be
a bee that tends
the honey store.

'We could go out and
forage for pollen in
flowers, nectar and water.

'Or we could
be a guard bee
for the hive.'

'None of those jobs seem to have any adventure in them,' Honey said and she slumped down in her wax seat.

Miss Ivy ignored Honey's comment. Well, she acted like she did anyway. She got up and looked down at Honey. 'Then we will give you a job in the hive that we feel best suits your skills.'

'But what if . . .' Honey started to say.

'You're a young bee, so let's try you out in the nursery looking after the larvae. We'll see how you do.'

'Are you sure you don't need an astronaut bee? I really think it's time we bees got into the space race, don't you agree . . .'

'You are dismissed.'

'To infinity and beyond . . .' Honey dramatically pointed to the sky.

Miss Ivy stared at her blankly. Then she

smiled, pointed to the door, and said, 'To the nursery and no farther!'

Honey shrugged and headed out towards the nursery. Maybe she could make taking care of the nursery larvae an adventure.

I mean, how hard could it be? she thought.

Her friend Beanie was already in the nursery. Beanie was short but sturdy, with fluffy fuzz and bright stripes on her thorax. She would make a great larvae nurse. She was like Mary Poppins but with a stinger. Honey had always known Beanie would end up here.

'Hey, Beanie!' Honey waved to her friend. 'What's the buzz? How's life with the larvae?'

'Hey, Honey!' Beanie fluttered over and the two bees tapped antennae. 'So glad you got assigned here too!' Beanie bounced excitedly. 'We can be bee worker buddies! Come on, I'll show you what to do. It's brilliant here. I'm definitely going to choose this as my job.'

Beanie showed Honey how to measure out the next feed for the larvae and tidy up the rows and rows of larvae cells. Honey didn't think it was as brilliant as Beanie had said and she started to sing to make it more fun. 'Whistle while you work,' she sang as she cleaned up. But when she tried to actually whistle, she just kind of buzzed and blew at the same time which covered the nursery and the larvae with bee spit.

(You see bees don't have lips. And you can't whistle with just your tongue. Try it. I'll wait . . . See?)

After they had cleaned the bee spit off the poor babies, Beanie left Honey with a row of sleeping larvae and went to deal with another row that had started to wake up.

'You OK with this group?' Beanie asked.

'Of course, I got this,' Honey answered, leaning back against a larvae crib. 'How hard can it be?'

A few hours later Honey stood caked in dried larvae sick, her eyes wide with shock and larvae goo dripping from her entire body (even her antennae). '*Hard*. Really, really hard,' she mumbled to herself.

Chapter 4

Ok, I'm going to rewind here.

This bit is just too good to skip. Even though we really do have to get to the part where things go wrong in the hive. I know you THINK that things are going wrong here for Honey but trust me, things are going to get a whole lot worse.

Which reminds me – let's get back to Honey.

'How hard can it be?' Honey asked, leaning against a larvae crib.

At first, the larvae all just looked so cute cuddled up in their little crib cells. 'Oh, bless them,' said Honey. 'They're so sweet.'

One of the larvae
started to squirm and
buzz-cry.

That set off another
of the larvae.

And then another.

'Right, they need feeding,' Honey said to
herself. 'Beanie showed me what to do. Easy.'

Honey picked up the larvae one at a time
and started drip feeding them honey like Beanie
had shown her. But it was taking so long. And
more and more were waking up now.

The noise of hundreds of larvae
'Bzzzahhhhhs!' filled the nursery.

Honey began to panic and started to feed the larvae faster. She noticed that they could actually suck down the honey pretty quickly, and the faster she fed one, the faster she could get on to the next one, so she sped up the feeding even more. Before long she started to feel like she was getting on top of it. The buzz-cries were dying down, but then the burping started. First one, then more. She picked up one and then two and then three of them to try and quiet them. *It can't hurt to try and rock and burp them like I've seen humans do to their babies*, she thought.

Honey was very very wrong.

All the honey that Honey had carefully fed the larvae now shot back out of the little creatures like tiny baby cannons of goo.

'Brrrraaaaaaaaapppppzzzzzzzzz!' was the noise of hundreds of baby bees all suddenly burping and spitting up at once.

It was not a sound often heard in a hive. It was not a sound any bee WANTED to hear in a hive. And it was definitely not a sound Honey ever EVER wanted to hear again.

Honey stood caked in crud, her eyes wide with shock and larvae goo dripping from her entire body (even her antennae).

'Taking care of larvae is hard. Really, really hard,' she mumbled to herself.

Beanie flew over and wiped off Honey's wings. 'Well, I think we can safely say that larvae nurse is probably not the worker bee job for you.'

'There are just sooooooo many of them.' Honey blinked and shook her head. 'And how can so much sick come out of such a little larva?'

'Yeah, I did try and tell you to drip feed them bit by bit. That happens when you feed them too much of the honey all at once,' Beanie answered. 'And, just so you know, burping a larva after feeding is NEVER a good idea.'

Beanie led Honey to a seat and handed her a hot cup of nectar.

'Drink this.'

As Honey drank, her mind flashed up images of the larvae vomit explosion and she shook her head.

'I'm sorry I messed up the nursery so much,' Honey said. 'I thought looking after the larvae might be fun. They would just look all cute and I'd find something that I was good at.'

'Being a larvae nurse isn't for everyone. But, Honey, and I mean this in the kindest possible way, I don't think I've ever seen a bee who was so bad at looking after the larvae.'

Honey nodded.

'Please don't pick this as your job.'

'Oh, don't worry. I won't,' Honey answered, her antennae drooping. 'But I'm no closer to finding a worker bee job that I'm any good at. What if I'm not good at anything?'

A little while later Honey was back in Miss Ivy's office.

'Didn't go too well at the nursery?' Miss Ivy said.

'I'm never allowed back in there apparently, so no, it didn't go very well.'

Miss Ivy got up and began to pace. She seemed quite distracted.

'I suppose you could clean the cells for now. Or put wax caps on the larvae cells, perhaps?'

'Not the larvae,' Honey said. 'Please not the larvae.'

Miss Ivy folded and unfolded her arms as she buzzed back and forth.

'Hmmmm.' She looked Honey up and down. 'Actually, there *is* a job that's come up – looking after the Queen,' she said. 'Normally, I would be more selective for this role but there has been a bit of difficulty . . .' she trailed off.

'I'm sure I can do that,' Honey said.

Looking after royalty would be way more interesting than looking after larvae.

The Queen was her mother after all. She could look after her.

'Please let me have a go,' Honey said. 'I won't try to burp the Queen. I promise.'

Miss Ivy flew over to the door and looked out. She peered left and then right down the corridor.

'You don't want to topple the monarchy or anything?' Miss Ivy asked, trying to sound casual but actually sounding a bit shaky.

'What? No, I like the Queen. She seems nice.'

'Oh, that's good, we'll head over to the throne room now then. I should probably accompany you, just in case.' Miss Ivy looked over her shoulder as they left the room and headed down the hall.

'Just in case of what?' Honey asked.

'Never mind. Perhaps this will all blow over,' Miss Ivy said, crossing all her arms again as she flew.

But things did not all 'blow over'. More blew *up* than blew over. But more on that in the next chapter.

Chapter 5

As soon as Honey and Miss Ivy left her office cell, Honey could feel something was different about the hive.

The other bees were rushing about, bumping into each other and shouting, 'Out of my way!' 'Can't you smell it?' 'It's happening.' All antennae were twitching. Stingers were out and ready and the bees just looked puffy and on edge.

Miss Ivy buzzed ahead of Honey, swishing through the throng of buzzing bees. 'We need to get past! Make way! Make way!' Miss Ivy demanded but the other bees didn't seem to take much notice.

Honey sniffed the air. 'What is that smell?' she asked Miss Ivy. 'I feel like it's trying to warn me about something.'

Miss Ivy tasted the air with her tongue. 'We need to hurry,' she said. 'There's not much time.'

In a short flight they arrived at the entrance to the royal chamber. There were a couple of very serious looking guard bees at the door, but they stepped aside as soon as they recognised Miss Ivy.

'Your Majesty,' Miss Ivy said and bowed her antennae on entering. She nudged Honey to do the same.

'Oh, yeah. Right,' Honey mumbled. 'Sorry.' Honey bobbed her antennae in a quick bow and then looked up and around the room. The Queen lay in the middle of the large chamber and folded and unfolded her arms. Attendants brushed at her furry middle, keeping her looking suitably smooth and preened for a queen.

Miss Ivy fluttered forward. 'May I present Honey, Your Majesty. Your newest helper.'

Honey's antennae twitched excitedly. 'Nice to meet you, Your Queenness.'

There was a pause. 'Oh, and I love your royal wave.' Honey did a demonstration of the Queen's many handed slow regal wave. It was a pretty good impression, actually.

Miss Ivy's eyes widened, and her wings started to twitch. She looked like she might pass out from shock. But a moment later the Queen smiled. 'Do you really? Like the wave, I mean? I practise it, you know. To get it just right.'

'It totally shows,' Honey replied.

As Miss Ivy flew over and started whispering to the Queen, Honey spotted a face she recognised peeping out from behind the Queen's enormous thorax.

'Hex?!' Honey shouted to her friend. 'What are you doing here?'

'I was going to ask you the same question,' Hex said.

Honey zoomed over and the two bumped antennae to say hi.

Hex handed Honey a brush. 'I was wondering what work experience they would give you, Honey.'

'I didn't expect this either, but I was terrible as a nursery bee and then Miss Ivy said there were some complications, so I needed to help out here.'

'Yeah, I was all set to help out the engineer bees building cells today, but they stopped building and sent me over here.' She looked around. 'I mean, looking after the Queen is an honour,' she whispered, 'but it's not really what I want to do.'

Honey nodded and brushed at the Queen's stripy fuzz.

'I did build the Queen a nice new wax lounge chair this morning, though,' Hex added.

The Queen then turned to her attendants. 'We are quite hungry.' Her big belly rumbled as if to make the point again. 'Might we have some more lunch?'

'I'm afraid not, Your Majesty,' Miss Ivy shook her head. 'They have fed you less on purpose for the last few days,' she explained. 'So you will be lighter to fly.' She paused. 'Just in case.'

A thud was heard in the passage outside the Queen's chamber. Honey flew over to the entrance to check it out. Bees were buzzing all over the place. And there was that smell again. The one that was trying to tell her something. But this time it was clearer. A word started to form in her head.

'SWARM.' She mumbled it to herself.
Miss Ivy flew over. 'What did you say?'

'Swarm,' Honey said. 'The smell.
It's saying "Swarm". What does that
mean?'

'It's begun, Your Majesty,' Miss Ivy said
to the Queen.

Just then Bella and some of her guards
burst into the chamber. Honey
jumped out of their way.

'Honey?' Bella said. 'You're safe!'

Then Bella turned and bowed to
the Queen. 'Your Majesty. We have
come to protect you in your escape.'

'Hang on,' Honey said,
grabbing one of Bella's arms.

'Why does the Queen need to
escape her own hive? What's going
on? And what is a swarm?'

49

Miss Ivy fluttered closer to the Queen and started to move her towards the entrance. 'It's a coup, Honey,' Miss Ivy explained. 'A new young queen is about to take over the hive.'

Bella added, 'If our Queen doesn't leave on her own, they will throw her out. We need to swarm with those loyal to our Queen and start a new hive somewhere else.' Bella's guards gathered around the Queen to protect her. 'We have to go now.'

Honey and Hex looked at each other. 'Beanie!' they both said.

Honey stood tall. 'We need to get Beanie!'

Chapter 6

'I said we have to go NOW,' Bella said, grabbing one of Honey's arms and pulling her towards the door.

Honey flapped away. 'We can't leave Beanie behind. We have to find her.' Hex flew over next to her.

'You can't risk it. It's safer if we all stay together,' Bella said.

'But we're not ALL together,' Honey said. 'We need to get Beanie. What did you used to call Beanie, Hex and me when we were little larvae? Do you remember?'

'Yes,' Bella said. 'Three bees in a pod. You were ALWAYS together.' She paused.

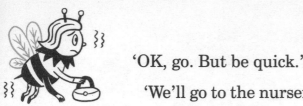

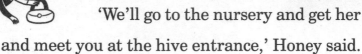

'OK, go. But be quick.'

'We'll go to the nursery and get her and meet you at the hive entrance,' Honey said.

Hex and Honey sped through the chaos of the hive. Bees were flying in every direction and the smell of fear and the urge to swarm and fly away were growing greater by the second.

When they got to the nursery Beanie was capping the larvae cells with wax as all the mayhem continued around her.

'Beanie, come on. We have to go,' Honey said, landing near her.

'I can't leave the larvae,' Beanie said. 'Who will look after them?'

'The new queen will want to look after the larvae to replenish the numbers after we all go,' Hex said. 'They'll be safe. Don't worry.'

'But we have to go now,' Honey said. 'You want to help the Queen, right? I mean she is our mother and all.'

'And she always seemed like a very nice Queen,' Beanie added.

'She's the only one I ever met,' Hex said. 'But she was very complimentary about the new lounge chair I made her this morning.'

'Oooh, you made her a lounge chair? Like a throne?' Beanie asked.

'OK look, can we not discuss how nice the Queen is and what her furniture is like when we are trying to escape from her rival queen,' Honey interrupted. 'The Queen is on the move and Bella and her guards can't wait for us much longer. Come on or we'll be left behind.'

The three young bees flew out of the nursery. Panic filled the hive now and Honey worried that they might meet the new young queen or her supporters around any corner. Honey had never had to fight in her life. Bella was the strong one. The guard bee. The one nobody messed with.

But Honey, Beanie and Hex on their own would be no match for some full-grown angry bees.

Finally, they approached the hive entrance. They could see Bella and her guards in a ball of bees herding the Queen towards the opening.

'I haven't flown in many seasons,' the Queen mumbled. 'What if I can't?'

Honey flew up next to her. 'It's just like waving with your wings, Your Majesty. You can do this. Just wave with your wings.'

In one final push the guards poured out of the hive with the Queen and all her swarm. Honey, Beanie and Hex flocked around the Queen as well to support her as she teetered on the edge of the platform outside the hive.

'We will wave with our wings,' the Queen mumbled to herself. 'Wave with our wings,' she repeated as she took off.

'That's it,' Honey shouted to her. 'You're flying.'

More and more bees tumbled out of the hive and joined the growing swarm.

Honey flew up to Bella at the front of the swarm.

'Where exactly are we going?' she asked her big sister.

'Anywhere but here for now,' Bella answered. 'We just need to get the Queen somewhere safe. Then who knows.'

Miss Ivy flew up next to them. 'We need to fly as far as the Queen can manage. We want some distance in case the new queen's supporters try to pursue us.'

'Understood!' Bella nodded. 'Honey – you, Hex and Beanie keep the Queen going. You can distract her as she flies so she doesn't notice the distance.'

'I'm on it,' Honey said and flew back to Hex and Beanie, who were buzzing along next to the Queen. She whispered Bella's plan to her friends. Beanie smiled and started chatting right away to the Queen.

'Your Majesty, have you heard about Honey's morning at the nursery today? You have never seen anything like it.'

While Beanie retold the embarrassing story of Honey's larvae vomit explosion (as it would now permanently be known) Honey looked around at the fields and houses below as the swarm swooped and soared away.

This was the furthest she had ever been in her short life. They were already far from everything she'd ever known. Her hive, her home, her friends. What would Nana Ladybird think when Honey didn't fly by tomorrow morning? What about Bob's cocoon? Or the ant family?

For the first time in her life Honey felt something new in the pit of her stomach. She was scared but it wasn't just fear. She was excited but it wasn't just that either. It was like the window on her world had been left a crack open and she'd flown out. But now she couldn't get back in again, although she could see that there was sooooo much to explore outside. Her tummy was a ball of emotions like . . . 'Scare-sitment' or 'Exci-fear.' A combination of excitement and fear that Honey felt like a rush of energy.

After all this time waiting – she was actually on an adventure.

Chapter 7

Now is a good time to pause, while everyone is swarming to wherever it is they are going.

There was an awful lot of 'bee stuff' in those last couple of chapters and I didn't want to stop to explain because it would break up the flow of the story. I know you are thinking, 'You do that all the time' and you would be right. But I wanted to keep things moving there. Just like Bella needed to keep the Queen moving until they got out of the hive.

OK, let's break down the bee stuff.

Firstly, the reason that Honey could smell a word in her head was that bees communicate with each other using smell. They send out smell signals to each other to pass on information. Sometimes it's everyday information like, 'Hey, I spotted a nice flower outside.' But sometimes it's important information like, 'There is going to be a swarm!!!!'

So, what is a swarm? Lots of people think that bees fly in a big group (called a swarm) because they are looking for something to attack. This is completely wrong. Actually, that is the last thing on a bee's mind when it's in a swarm. Bees swarm from a hive because they have to leave it or their queen will be thrown out. It's an escape - not an attack at all.

I know what you're thinking. How could there be a new queen when I said that there is only one queen in a hive? OK, I fudged that bit when I explained it before. What I should have said is that usually there is only one queen in the hive but SOMETIMES a new queen is born, and she grows up and gets strong and then comes out of her cell fighting and ready to take over. That sends a smell message to the other bees, and they basically pick a side. They either back the new queen and take over or they support the old queen and swarm with her.

Honey, Bella, Hex, Beanie, Miss Ivy, and this swarm now have the extremely difficult job of keeping the Queen safe, finding a new hive, and rebuilding their colony. Honey was right. This was certainly going to be an adventure.

So, let's get back to our bees.

'We are quite tired now,' the Queen gasped.

'Are you sure there isn't a bit more wave left in those wings?' Honey asked.

The Queen smiled but her wings beat slower and slower. 'Not much, I'm afraid.'

Honey flew up to speak to Bella. Bella was one of the fastest flyers, so she was way out in front leading the swarm. It was all Honey could do to catch up.

'I think the Queen is really tired,' Honey said. 'Probably lots of the bees are by now, actually. Is there anywhere we can land for the night?'

Bella looked back at the swarm. The pace of their flight had definitely slowed in the last couple of hours. 'Maybe we can find a tree to stop in?' she suggested.

Honey looked around. There weren't any fields nearby now. Just more and more houses that were close together and tall, tall buildings that reached up into the sky. Higher than the trees. There *was* a small shed at the edge of a garden beneath them though, that had its door open.

'I'm going to check that out,' Honey said, and she dived down to look. The shed was dark but sheltered and had a sink in it with water dripping from the tap. Honey thought, *The Queen must be parched by now and will need a drink*. Honey certainly did. This looked like a safe place to stop.

She flew back up and pointed it out to Bella. Bella looked back at the Queen, who was slowing with every wingbeat. 'OK, let's stop here.'

Bella led the swarm down to the shed and inside. There were no animals or humans about.

It looked quiet and most importantly they could rest and drink.

'This will do nicely for the night,' Miss Ivy said to Bella as she flitted onto the top of the tap to rest. 'Good choice.'

'Honey spotted it actually,' Bella said, still buzzing around making sure everyone was inside the shed.

'Hmmm. That young bee is certainly full of surprises.' Miss Ivy nodded and sent out some of the forager bees to look for nectar while Hex and Beanie helped the Queen to have a drink.

Honey fluttered out and landed on the shed roof. She looked around at the garden. This place was very different from home. It was certainly noisier. The sounds of traffic crawling down the roads filled Honey's ears and drowned out any birdsong. Dogs barked from inside houses and people shouted to each other on the street and from behind windows. Why was everything so loud here?

It smelled different too. Not so much the smell of grass and flowers but more the smells of cars and of humans cooking whatever it was they ate.

Then Honey heard a very familiar sound. A buzz. A bee buzz. But it wasn't from inside the shed. It was from the wooden fence that separated the gardens. Honey followed the sound.

Chapter 8

As Honey flew near the fence, she could see the familiar yellow and black stripes of a bee. He was bigger than Honey; about as large as the Queen. But he didn't look like a queen. He was rounder and was moving much quicker than the Queen did. He buzzed in and out of the hole in his wooden fence, tidying and fussing about. But he seemed to be on his own. A bee on his own? Where was his hive? In all the weirdness of today, this was the strangest thing yet.

After noticing Honey buzzing around for a minute or two the lone bee finally turned to Honey and spoke.

'Good evening, young bee,' he said, nodding his head. 'So, are you going to land and say hello or just buzz around all night?'

'Um . . . Hello.' Honey was at a loss for words (and that NEVER happened). 'Um,' she repeated.

'I don't sting.' The lone bee smiled and then laughed. 'Heck, I can't sting. Don't have a stinger.'

Honey landed on a fence post next to him. 'Um . . .' she started.

'Yup. You said that.' He smiled again. 'Come on. Spit it out.'

'You're on your own? You're a bee and you're on your own. Where's your hive? Where's your queen? Where's your family?' Honey just let the questions spill out of her now.

'I don't have a hive. Don't need one.' He tapped the wood of the fence. 'I've got my nest in this hole in the wood. That's all I need.'

Honey stayed quiet for a full minute, taking that in. He had no hive. No queen to look after. No family to tell him what to do. It was just him. A bee on his own.

Then she suddenly blurted out. 'Oh my buzzness, that's amazing!!!'

'It's pretty ordinary for a carpenter bee actually,' he said. 'And that's what I am. I'm Carl. Pleased to meet you.' He paused and waited but Honey didn't get the hint that he expected her to introduce herself too. She was still too blown away by the idea of a bee living alone.

Carl continued. 'And you are?'

'Oh, yes, sorry. I'm Honey.' She fluttered up and buzzed around as she talked. 'I'm in a swarm that's resting in the shed over there. Our Queen got pushed out of our hive. It's pretty far from here. Anyway, we are really tired, and the Queen is completely exhausted so we had to take a break and rest here. But I got bored and came out and that's when I heard you buzzing and thought, *Hmmm that sounds like a bee. Wonder if there's another hive around here?* and then I saw you and saw you were on your own and not in a hive and that is just the strangest but most wonderful thing I've ever heard.'

'You go straight from "um" to that?' Carl said. 'Phew. Take a breath, young bee. Relax.

If you are here to rest, then maybe it would be a good idea to actually rest.' He pulled over a piece of wood chip for Honey to sit on.

'Oh, thanks,' she said. 'So, why do you live alone? I'm sorry to be nosy. My teachers always say I ask too many questions. You can tell me to stop if you want.'

'Somehow I don't think that would work but thanks for offering.' Carl smiled. 'I live alone because that's what carpenter bees do. We dig out wood to make our own nests. We forage for ourselves and keep to ourselves most of the time. We get together sometimes but most of the season we are on our own.' He paused. 'And that suits me fine.'

'I think I would LOVE that!' Honey said.

'Do you really?' Carl asked. 'Because I think you might miss talking to other bees. This is the most conversation I've had in months. Don't get me wrong, it's lovely to speak with you, but you are used to talking a lot with friends and family, right?'

Honey nodded.

'Are they in the swarm with you?' Carl asked.

'Yes, and this has been the most exciting,

most scary, but most adventurous day I've ever had,' Honey said. 'I was supposed to pick my worker bee job today but instead I'm now out in the world in search of a new home. It's just . . .' Honey trailed off.

'It's just what?' Carl said.

'When we find a new hive, it will all go back to normal. I'll be expected to get a worker bee job and be a good bee and there will be no more adventures.'

'What do you think a "good bee" is?' Carl asked.

Honey straightened up and saluted.

'A bee must . . .

Bee loyal, bee strong.

You must always get along.

Bee considerate, bee kind.

Work hard and you'll find

Your place in the hive.

You'll help it survive.

Together, you see,

You can be your best bee.'

'Wow,' Carl said. 'That's a mouthful and a half.' He paused. 'There are some nice ideas in there though.'

'But what is my place in the hive? Why am I responsible for helping all the time? Why do I always have to do what everyone else says?'

'Big questions for a little bee,' Carl said

and thought. 'But, short answer, you don't.'

'I don't what?' Honey said.

'Have to do what everyone else says. You are your own bee,' Carl said. 'I just think you would miss the good stuff that comes from having a—'

'Of course I'm my own bee. And if I want to fly off into the sky and explore, I will because I'm my own bee,' Honey said.

'You CAN do that BUT—' Carl started again.

'Thanks, Carl. I'm off to explore. Can't keep me down,' she said and took to the air.

'No, I didn't think I could. Just stay safe, little bee.' He waved and got back to moving his sawdust off his ledge.

Honey zoomed into the evening sky. The light was fading, and the moon rose in the sky. Honey had never been out this late in the day. And she'd never felt so alive.

She headed out of the garden and towards one of the really tall buildings they had around there. But as she got closer, she heard buzzing again. But this buzzing was different. It wasn't honeybees or a lone carpenter bee. It was . . .

'Wasps!' Honey gasped.

Chapter
9

Now you might think that wasps and bees are sort of the same. But they are very different.

Wasps and honeybees are about the same size, but honeybees are built for gathering nectar and buzzing from flower to flower - round and fuzzy. Wasps are hunters and they are built for speed with sleek bullet-shaped bodies. They will attack and raid a hive if they think they can steal food and they will attack a lone bee if it seems vulnerable. And, for once in her life, Honey was a lone bee.

'Right, what did Bella tell me to do if I was ever chased by a wasp? Find her? . . . OK, well that's not an option . . .'

Honey buzzed over the fence and towards

the big building, thinking desperately what to do. Maybe she could lose the wasps.

She remembered Bella practising drills with her guard bees. 'Evasive manoeuvres!' She would shout. Honey wasn't entirely sure what that meant but she was pretty sure it was something like zigzag around a lot so they can't follow you.

(Hint – Honey was right. That's exactly what it means.)

Honey zigged and she zagged, but the wasps were still gaining on her. Then she spotted some sliding doors open at the bottom of the building.

Maybe I can hide in there? she thought to herself and flew inside.

'Ahhhhhhhhhh!' shouted a very surprised-looking fly who was already inside the small room behind the doors.

'Ahhhhhhhhhh!' Honey shouted back at the fly.

This could have gone on for ages. Both Honey and this particular fly were a bit dramatic. But fortunately, Honey remembered the wasps.

'Wasps!' she shouted to the fly instead.

'Wasps?' he shouted back.

'Wasps!' she answered. 'They're coming this way.'

'Why would you bring wasps into the lift with you?' the fly asked.

'What's a lift?' Honey asked back as a little button on the wall went *PING* and lit up and the sliding doors closed just before the wasps reached them. She could hear the muffled sound of wasps bouncing off the now closed doors outside. *Boiiinnnggg! Boiiinnnggg!*

'Did you do that?' Honey asked the fly. 'Because if you did, that was perfect timing.'

'I didn't. Sorry,' he answered. 'I can't push the buttons. Someone must have pressed a button upstairs.'

Then the whole room began to move. Honey had never been in a moving room before.

The fly noticed that Honey was feeling a little uneasy. Perhaps it was the fact that her antennae were twitching faster than a hummingbird's wings. Or maybe it was the way she shrieked and clung to the wall shouting, 'HELP.'

Anyway, he tried to calm her down. 'We'll be at the top soon. Unless it breaks down. Sometimes it breaks down on the way.'

This just resulted in her shouting again.

'AHHHHHHHHHHHHHHHHHH!'

But Honey's panic was surprisingly short-lived as before long the little glowing button on the wall made another *PING* and the doors slid open again.

A human lady with a large sunhat and glasses looked a little shocked to see a fly and a bee zoom out of the lift before she got in.

The doors closed behind Honey and the fly and Honey looked around. She was in a garden. *Impossible,* thought Honey. This magic room had taken them to a garden. And it was beautiful.

'Welcome to the roof garden,' the fly said. 'Oh, sorry, my name is Fred.'

'Wow,' Honey said, buzzing around the garden.

'It's not that impressive a name really . . .' Fred said.

'No, sorry. Not WOW about your name.

I mean, Fred is a nice name but not a WOW.'

'Agreed,' he said.

'Just WOW about this garden. Where are we?' Honey said, still swooping from plant to plant and bench to trellis.

'And you are?' he said.

'I keep forgetting to do that,' she paused. 'I'm Honey. I'm a bee,' she added. 'And are you a housefly?'

'I'm a flatfly,' Fred said. 'I don't live in a house; I live in a flat, so I think that's more accurate. I like to be accurate.'

'Pleasure to meet you. This place is amazing. Much bigger than the cottage garden. But where are we? Where is the building where I came in?'

'You're on top of it. This is the rooftop garden of the block of flats. It's really high up. Lots of people use this garden to plant vegetables and flowers and lots of insects live here.'

There were large planters all along the roof edge full of geraniums, tulips, peonies and roses. There was a trellis on the walls and jasmine and ivy growing up the sides. There were also vegetable planters and some that just had dirt. Maybe they hadn't been planted up yet.

A couple of benches were off to one side and a table and chairs were grouped on the other. There was a patch of grass in the middle. Honey landed on it. It didn't feel like grass. It felt like the plastic straws that were in human drinks sometimes. Fake grass?

'"Astro turf" they call it,' Fred explained. 'So they don't have to mow the grass.'

'Humans are weird.' Honey shook her antennae.

'Yes, but they do also make some great food,' Fred said. 'Especially the lady three floors down, second window on the right. Oh, and the men in the balcony flat. Oh my buzzness, their cakes are worth being nearly swatted for.'

Fred seemed to drift off for a second, remembering the cakes. Honey decided to leave him in his cake dream and look around more. And that's when she spotted the wooden box in the corner of the roof garden.

She flew over and had a closer look.

'It's a hive!' she squealed.

'Oh, a beehive? Is that what it is?' Fred asked.

'We need to look inside!' A glint came to Honey's eyes. The kind of glint that happened when she was just about to embark on something slightly risky. Something that she probably shouldn't do if she was being sensible, but Honey was not known for being sensible.

Like when she got Hex and Beanie to help her make a bee trampoline out of some old spider web. That was a sticky situation. But that's another story.

She grabbed one of Fred's arms and dragged him to the entrance of the hive. The wood was a bit rotten in places, the paint was chipped off and the roof was definitely wonky.

'Helllllloooooo! Anyone home?'

Honey shouted into the entrance.

'No bees?' Fred said, looking in. 'Or anything else?'

'What else would be in there?' Honey said.

'I don't know.' Fred shrugged.

Chapter 10

Honey pulled Fred into the hive, and they looked around.

'This is a pretty good size for a hive, I think,' Honey said. 'I mean I've only lived in one hive, but it seems about the same size.'

'I've never been in a hive so I really wouldn't know,' Fred said.

'Maybe we could move here?' Honey bounced up and down in the air. 'We could live in this hive? In this garden?' she said. 'I have to get Beanie and Hex. They'll know what to do.' She fluttered out of the hive and Fred followed.

Honey flew to the edge of the roof and looked down. She couldn't see the shed from this side. She zoomed over to the other edge of the roof. There it was – very small in the distance. And a long way down.

Honey turned and waved to Fred. 'See you soon. I'm going to bring my friends to see the abandoned hive.' She buzzed off the roof and headed for the shed below.

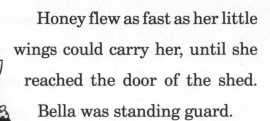

Honey flew as fast as her little wings could carry her, until she reached the door of the shed. Bella was standing guard.

'Where've you been?' Bella wagged her antennae at Honey as soon as she landed. 'You can't just fly off whenever you feel like it.'

'I'm fine. And I *can* just fly off as it happens . . .' Honey started to say but then stopped herself. 'Look, it's a good thing I did fly off, I might have found something important. Where are Hex and Beanie?'

'They're inside. They're actually doing a really good job distracting the Queen, so she doesn't get too freaked out by all this change,' Bella admitted.

'I'll be back in a bit.' Honey started to fly inside but then stopped and gave her sister a sudden hug. 'Sorry I worried you. But I'm OK when I just fly off, you know.' Then she headed inside to see Beanie and Hex.

When Miss Ivy took over chatting to the Queen about pollen collection schedules and stuff to distract her, the three friends managed to sneak out.

Once outside Honey flew over the fence and motioned for Hex and Beanie to follow. 'You're not going to believe what I found,' Honey said. 'I want you both to see it first, before I tell any of the swarm. Can you keep a secret?'

Beanie and Hex nodded.

'Then come on,' Honey said.

The three bees flew up through the night sky, past the lit-up windows from the flats in the tower block. They stopped for a moment at the balcony flat on the seventh floor because of the smell of hazelnut chocolate cake coming from the open window. Honey made a note to let Fred know that there was fresh cake around.

When they reached the top, they all collapsed by a puddle on the roof in an exhausted fuzzy bee pile and sipped at the water.

'I didn't know they made buildings this big!' Beanie said.

'Basic engineering principles,' Hex said. 'Same as we build big structures for our hives or termites build a big hill to live in.'

Then Hex looked around at the garden. 'But, oh my buzzness, it's not just a building, there's a garden on top?' she said.

'We're in a garden in the sky,' Beanie squealed.

'I know!' Honey said. 'It's amazing. But that's not the best bit.'

Honey flew them over to the entrance of the abandoned hive. Fred was waiting for them.

'Hi, I'm Fred and I'll be your guide for the evening,' he said.

Honey giggled. 'My friends, Hex and Beanie, would like a full tour of the hive please,' she said.

'It's a great location,' Fred smiled.

The four of them buzzed into the hive and explored from floor to roof and looked at all the slats and tunnels and all the space for making honeycomb cells for the swarm.

'So, what do you think?' Honey finally asked.

'It's in pretty good shape,' Hex said, tapping the wall with her stinger. 'It's old and a bit run-down but I think we could make it really nice.'

'I can see right away where I would put the nursery,' Beanie said. 'Oh, and the Queen's throne room could be there. And the drones could have their chambers there.' She spun around the place, imagining all the changes they could make.

'So, do you think we could convince everyone to move in here? Could we convince the Queen?' Honey asked.

They flew out of the entrance and landed on the roof of the hive together. Hex looked over the edge of the building.

'I think the hive is great, Honey. I can't believe you found us a potential new home,' Hex said.

'I did have a bit of help.' Honey bumped Fred with her tail.

Then Hex looked over the side again. 'But it's so far up.'

Beanie flew to the roof edge and peered over. 'Hex is right. It's so far up. The Queen . . .'

Honey's antennae flopped down as she realised. 'The Queen could never fly up here.' She slumped down against the slatted roof.

'Maybe if we gave her a boost?' Beanie tried to sound optimistic, but the others all shook their heads.

'It's no good,' Honey said. 'She is not built to fly that much. She just can't do that height. She's too big and too tired. We'll have to find another home.'

'I'm sure there'll be a hollow tree? Or something somewhere we can use,' Beanie offered.

They all sat in silence looking out at the sky when suddenly their sulk was disturbed by the *PING* of the lift doors opening again. A couple walked out of the lift and sat down on one of the benches.

Honey jumped up. 'That's it! We'll bring the Queen up in the lift! We'll bring the *whole swarm* up in the lift!'

'What's a lift?' Hex and Beanie asked together.

'It's easier to show you. Come on,' Fred said, and they all zoomed towards the doors and flew in just before the sliding doors pinged shut again.

'Now this is going to feel a bit weird,' Honey told them as the room started to go down.

'Ahhhhhhhhhhhhhhhhhhh!'

Hex and Beanie shouted together all the way down in the lift to the ground floor. They only stopped when the doors made the *PING* sound again and opened.

Fred, Honey, Beanie and Hex all zoomed out, terrifying a man who was carrying several bags of groceries.

'The room?' Beanie said. 'It moved????'

'How did it do that?' Hex asked. 'I have to find out.'

'I actually have no idea,' Honey said. 'But the moving room can take us from the ground right up to the roof garden.'

'We have to tell Miss Ivy,' Beanie said.

'And the Queen!' Hex added.

'Come on,' Honey said.

Chapter 11

Fred was about to take off with them when he sniffed the air. 'Chocolate hazelnut?' he mumbled.

'Oh, yeah, I forgot to tell you. Seventh floor, guys with the balcony,' Honey said. 'It smelled really good.'

'I might have to ummmm . . .' Fred started.

'Investigate?' Honey finished his sentence. 'No worries. We'll head back, do a waggle dance to show everyone where to go and then bring the swarm in the morning.'

'We'd better get back quick,' Hex said. 'Bella will be super worried by now.'

'OK, See you later, Fred,' Honey said and

the three young bees zoomed back towards the shed.

As they passed into the garden, they flew over Carl, who was working on his nest.

'Oh, there's someone else I want you guys to meet,' Honey said and flew down.

'Hi, Carl.' Honey waved as she landed in front of him. Beanie and Hex fluttered down behind her.

'Hi,' they both said together. 'Are you a new drone bee in our hive?' Hex asked. 'I don't think I've seen you before.'

'I'm not a drone,' Carl said. 'I'm not even a honeybee. I'm a carpenter bee. Carl's the name. Pleased to meet you,' he nodded.

'So where are the rest of the bees in your hive, Carl?' Beanie asked, looking around.

'It's just me. On my own.' Carl smiled. Beanie and Hex stared.

'I know! But we don't have time to explain it all now,' Honey said to Hex and Beanie. 'Carl, we've found the most amazing hive to move into. It's on the rooftop of that big building,' she said.

Carl looked up at the top of the tower block. 'That's a mighty high-up place to put a hive,' he said. 'But each to his own.'

'We were a bit worried about getting the Queen up there,' Hex said.

'But then we rode in the moving room,' Beanie explained.

'Fred called it a lift. Do you know what a lift is, Carl?' Hex asked.

'Nope. Can't say that I do. I'll just add that to the long list of stuff that I don't know.'

He looked around at the ground. 'That is if I can find the list.' He shrugged. 'Oh well.'

Then he turned to Honey. 'This new hive sounds interesting.'

'It'll give us a home,' Beanie said. 'Somewhere to put the larvae. That's the important thing.'

'And it's going to be a big building project.

Lots of stuff to design and build. That's exciting,' Hex added.

'And, Honey, does the hive have what you wanted?' Carl asked.

'I don't know,' Honey said. 'I don't even know if I can get what I want.'

'The dung beetle doesn't wait for the dung to come to her,' Carl said and looked knowingly at the young bees.

Beanie and Hex smiled awkwardly.

'So . . . Honey wants dung?' Beanie whispered. 'Is that what he means?'

'I mean that the dung beetle doesn't wait for the dung to come to her,' Carl said again. 'You have to go out and get what you want. Not wait for it to come to you.'

'Is there dung coming here?' Beanie whispered. 'I'd rather not be here when it comes if that's OK. I have a very sensitive sense of smell.'

'I think I get it.' Honey smirked. 'There's no dung, Beanie. You're OK. Let's get back to the shed before Bella sends out a search party.'

The three young bees took off. 'Thanks, Carl,' Honey shouted back.

Just in case you didn't know, 'dung' is animal poo. Dung beetles collect it and eat it. The animal world is vast and complex and has a lot of poo in it so somebody might as well make use of it. Oh, and there are definitely times when the dung beetle does wait for the dung to come to her. Like when she is standing behind the rhino. But that's another story and one that doesn't smell particularly nice. Back to Honey and her friends.

'What was all that about?' Hex asked Honey as they flew back.

'I don't think I'm any closer to knowing what I want to be as a worker bee. Or even if I want to be a worker bee,' Honey said. 'All I know is that the last day has been the most exciting time I've had in my life. I want to find a home for us all, but I want adventure. I don't think I want that excitement to end.'

'HONEY!' Bella shouted from outside the shed as they approached.

'I think you're about to get some excitement, Honey,' Hex said and peeled back to fly behind Honey, letting her land first on the step of the shed.

Chapter 12

'I was getting a search party together for you three!' Bella zoomed down and stood over Honey. 'Anything could have happened to you out there.'

'And it did!' Honey bounced excitedly. 'We've found a new place to live. I showed it to Hex and Beanie and they agree. It could be our new home.'

Bella's frown softened. 'Really?'

'Really,' Beanie and Hex said together.

'The Queen is still very tired,' Bella said. 'I hope it's not far. Can you do a waggle dance to show everyone the way?'

'Well, it's not that close, but we have a plan,' Honey said.

They all went inside and gathered in front of the swarm of bees. Miss Ivy and the Queen were watching too.

Beanie, Hex and Honey all started to do their waggle dance to tell the other bees about what they had found.

If you haven't heard of a waggle dance, it's a unique bee thing. Some animals do a dance to attract a mate or to show off to potential rivals. But honeybees do a dance to show each other the way to get to places. It's like a dancing version of a sat nav, really.

Hex, Beanie and Honey had of course learned how to do a waggle dance pretty well in Bee School. Honey hadn't had as much practice though because during an early waggle dance lesson Honey remembered something that she'd seen some human kids doing called 'break dancing.' So instead of doing a dance to direct her fellow bee students to the nearest sunflower she'd ended up doing a head spin that flipped into a windmill. Let's just say, it didn't end well. With legs, antennae and wings everywhere, Honey knocked over half the class before Miss Ivy could stop her. Honey had had to sit out and watch the practices after that.

So, Beanie and Hex each did a waggle to show heading out over the fence and along the road, then they indicated flying into the building. The other bees looked a bit confused.

'How do we show the moving room,' Hex whispered to Honey.

'Ah,' Honey jumped up. 'I've got this.'

Honey broke into some of her previous break-dancing moves. She spun around to show the swarm all forming into a ball and then . . .

'They call this a moonwalk, I think,' Honey said and moonwalked back and forth to show the sliding doors opening and closing on the lift.

Then Hex, Beanie and Honey all did a very shaky and waggly dance where they levitated up.

The three bees all juddered to a stop. Then, Honey moonwalked again to show the lift doors opening.

Beanie, Hex and Honey all did waggle dance moves specific to the flowers and plants that were on the roof. Roses, geraniums, ivy, and jasmine.

Lastly, they did the waggle dance move that meant home.

The other bees all clapped but the expressions on their faces looked like they were trying to figure out what they had just watched.

'Good effort, girls.' Miss Ivy stepped forward. 'This place sounds lovely with all those plants and flowers. It sounds a bit far to go to forage though to then head home at the end . . .'

'No,' Honey interrupted. 'I think we used the wrong waggle for the end. We don't go back to our old hive. The end is maybe our new home. We've found a new hive.'

Hex spoke up. 'It's an abandoned hive,' she said.

'It's got lots of room for a nursery and throne room . . .' Beanie started.

'And plenty of room to build,' Hex added.

Bella stepped forward. 'I followed most of your directions but what was that sliding bit you did, Honey?'

'This.' Miss Ivy attempted to do a moonwalk, but it didn't quite work.

'Oh, that was supposed to show the lift,' Honey said. 'The garden is on the top of a tall building.'

Beanie added: 'We need the swarm to ride up in the moving room.'

'It sounds dangerous,' Miss Ivy said. 'I'm not sure if Her Majesty . . .'

'Her Majesty will do what needs to be done.' A regal sounding voice came from the crowd.

The bees parted and the Queen stepped forward. 'If these young bees have really found our swarm a new home, we will follow them into their . . .' she paused and whispered to Honey. 'What did you call it?'

'A lift, Your Majesty,' Honey said.

'We will follow them into their lift to get to our hive,' the Queen continued.

'But Your Majesty, we should be practical. It might be risky. We shouldn't take the chance,' Miss Ivy said.

Bella stepped forward again. 'I believe in Honey. She wouldn't suggest it if she didn't think we could do it. If she didn't think that *you* could do it, Your Majesty.'

'I agree,' the Queen said. 'Let us prepare to leave at first light.'

Chapter
13

The next morning as the sun rose, Honey, Hex and Beanie all led the way towards the new hive. Bella and her team of guard bees followed closely around the Queen, keeping watch for anything out of the ordinary. The swarm headed out over the fence, past Carl's nest. He waved to the young bees as they flew by.

'Good Luck, Honey!' he shouted.

As they neared the end of the driveway to the tower block Honey started to feel something. It was a danger scent like she had felt before they left the hive. Before they swarmed.

Bella flew up next to her. 'Do you feel it too?' Bella said. 'Something just doesn't smell right.'

That's when they heard it. The buzzing.

'Wasps!' Honey and Bella said at the same time.

'Oh no, the wasps are still here,' Honey said.

'Still here?' said Bella. 'You didn't think to mention there were wasps on the way to your new hive!'

'I'm sorry. I didn't see them after the first time I went out yesterday. I thought they were gone.'

'They *were* gone, Honey,' Bella said. 'The second time you went out was late at night, remember. Of course, they weren't around then!'

'I didn't think of that. I'm sorry,' Honey said.

'Never mind. We have to protect the Queen,' Bella said. 'Evasive manoeuvres!' she shouted to her guard bees. 'Let's make the swarm a

moving target that is seriously hard to catch. We'll engage with the wasps and distract them, while Honey and her friends get the Queen and the others and hide. But be careful, Honey. The attack wasps will be able to track your scent.'

Bella and her guard bees peeled off away from the swarm and zigzagged to draw off the wasps who were heading towards them. It seemed to work and they distracted the wasps, but for how long?

Hex and Beanie flew up next to Honey. 'What can we do to help?'

'I don't know,' Honey said. 'I shouldn't have brought everyone here. Now the Queen is in danger and it's my fault.'

'Don't wait for the dung to come to you,' Beanie said.

'What do you mean?' Honey asked.

'I don't really know but it sounded really wise when Carl said it so I thought I would say it again.'

Then a little lightbulb went off in Honey's head. And by that, I mean that she had an extraordinary idea.

'That's it,' Honey shouted. 'We can't wait for the dung to come to us.'

'I don't think there is actual dung around . . .' Hex said. 'I would smell it.'

'Exactly, we would smell it. And the wasps

smell us and know that we are vulnerable. But what if we confused what they smelled?' Honey said.

'OK, but we can't fly over a pile of dung or something because there is no pile of dung,' Hex said.

'But there is rubbish. Lots of human rubbish. The bins for the flats. Look!' Honey pointed to the area by the doors to the entrance of the tower block. The smell from the bins was super strong. It would definitely overpower any scent from the bees.

Honey flew over to the Queen and Miss Ivy. 'I have a plan. It might mean getting a little messy but trust me it'll be worth it.'

Honey, Hex and Beanie led the Queen, Miss Ivy and the other bees over to the bins and they hid in the rubbish. They stayed still and quiet and hoped that once the wasps had finished fighting with Bella and her guards, they would give up and not find the swarm.

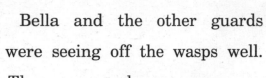

Bella and the other guards were seeing off the wasps well. There were only a few wasps left still flying around near the entrance to the tower block.

'We can't make a break for the tower block with those wasps there. Once they pick up our scent or see us, they'll tell the others. But we can't hide in the rubbish for ever.'

'I don't know. It's one of my favourite places to hide really,' a voice said from underneath a cupcake wrapper.

'Fred?' Honey said.

'You made it back. And this must be your swarm. Wow. There's a lot of you,' Fred said. 'Hello, everyone.'

The Queen looked rather surprised at being addressed by a fly.

'So did you just decide to take a break in the rubbish?' asked Fred. 'Nice choice. Can I recommend the sweet wrappers? But don't fly into the cola cans, it can be tricky to get out again.'

'Fred. We need your help,' Honey said.

'Of course, what can I do?'

'I need you to lead the swarm into the lift and get them to the roof. Hex and Beanie can go with you to help keep everybody together,' Honey said.

'Sure. But what are *you* going to do?'

'I'm going to distract those last few wasps.'

Chapter 14

Honey picked up a shiny sweet wrapper and flew off. The wrapper glinted in the sun and the last three wasps noticed her right away. It might have also helped that at the same time she was wildly shouting, 'Wooo hoo! Hey, you wasps over there!!! Look at me!!!!'

Honey was not subtle.

Honey flew up and away from the building to lead the wasps away from the door. They chased after her. Yes! Her plan was working. Now Fred, Hex and Beanie would be able to lead the swarm into the lift and up to the safety of the new hive.

There was only one problem with Honey's

plan. It now meant that Honey was being chased by three rather mean-looking wasps and they were gaining on her.

Bella and her guard bees were just heading back to find the swarm when Bella saw Honey and her flashing silver sweet wrapper in the distance.

'*What is she doing*?' Bella asked herself (knowing full well that the answer from herself was 'probably some wild crazy plan that is going to get her in trouble.') Because to be honest, that is mostly what happened to Honey.

Bella spotted the rest of the swarm slowly moving from the bins over to the entrance of the building. 'The Queen and swarm are on the move,' she shouted to the other guard bees. 'Go and protect them! I have to check on Honey.'

The other guard bees headed down to the entrance and helped herd the bees inside.

They just had to wait for the lift now and hope it would arrive before the wasps doubled back and saw them.

Meanwhile, Honey kept flying.

Maybe I can outrun them? she thought to herself, panting. *Maybe they'll just get bored and give up?* she added, trying to convince herself as she thought it.

When she turned around to look, though, the wasps were even closer and they showed no sign of looking bored or giving up. In fact, they looked very fierce and scarier than the last time she looked.

But Honey also spotted a bee coming up quickly behind the wasps. Who was that?

Bella? Oh my buzzness! Bella!

Bella buzzed past the wasps and flew up beside Honey.

'Hi!' Honey said.

'Hi?' Bella shouted. 'You are being chased by a bunch of wasps after I specifically told you to stay and hide with the swarm – and all you can say is "Hi"?'

'Oh yeah, um . . . Sorry, sis, I had a plan. I needed to lure the wasps away from the swarm,' Honey said, turning towards Bella as she flew.

'Honey! Duck!' Bella yelled.

'Where is the duck, I don't see a . . . ?' Honey turned around to look but then immediately dipped down to avoid a tree branch. 'Ahhhhhhhh!'

'Phew. Oh, you meant duck out of the way, not a *quack quack* kind of duck,' Honey said, panting.

'You need to look where you're flying Honey,' Bella said. 'Keep your eyes on the skies.'

'OK, but that's a little tricky when I'm looking back all the time to see how close the wasps are.'

'Then let's try and lose these wasps,' Bella said. 'Follow my lead.'

Bella banked hard to the left and swooped down. Then she zoomed straight up and to the right. Honey stayed close but she was struggling to match Bella's speed.

Unfortunately, the wasps were keeping up as well.

'They are still right behind us,' Bella said.

'So much for my plan,' Honey groaned.

'Well, it worked in that the swarm is safe. But now, we are both being chased by wasps, and we can't go back or they'll follow us, and we can't slow down or they'll catch us!'

'I guess I hadn't really thought it through,' said Honey.

'Sometimes your bright ideas are genius and sometimes they are big, big trouble.'

Just as Bella's words floated over Honey's antennae, she was distracted by something shimmering in the tree branch to the side of them. It was a spider's web that was damp with dew and glistening in the sun.

'I think I just got one of my bright ideas!' Honey shouted.

'Genius or trouble?' Bella asked.

'Probably a bit of both,' Honey admitted.

'Do you remember when I tried to make the spider web trampoline at school?' Honey asked.

'Yes, it was less of a bouncy trampoline and more of a sticky, gooey net. It took ages for your class at Bee School to chew their way out of it,' Bella said.

Honey pointed to the spider web. 'Exactly.'

'Oh my buzzness,' Bella agreed. 'Let's try it.'

Chapter
15

Bella and Honey flew to either end of the web where it was attached to the branches and snipped the ties with their jaws. Then grabbed the edges of the web and flew.

The web billowed out between them and slowed them down.

Now the wasps were getting closer by the second. They were almost right behind them. Honey looked over at Bella and shouted, 'Now!'

Bella and Honey pulled the web net as wide as they could and then suddenly stopped dead, hovering in the air as the wasps sped towards them.

The wasps' eyes widened as they approached
but they couldn't stop in time. The three wasps
barrelled into the web net and were immediately
stuck in the sticky threads.

'Gotcha!!!' Honey shouted.

Bella and Honey flew, lugging the net of
wasps over to a branch and stuck it to a tree. The
wasps flailed and raged, trying to free themselves
but only managed to cover themselves in more
sticky threads.

'It should take them a while to cut
themselves out of that,' Bella said. 'Come on.
We need to get back to the others.'

Bella and Honey flew back towards the building. They could see the ball of bees in the swarm still waiting with Fred in the entrance where the sliding doors to the lift were.

'Looks like the moving room hasn't moved yet,' Bella said. 'Those wasps will cut themselves free soon and when they do, they'll head this way. And bring more wasps with them.'

'Maybe we need to get someone from the sky garden to press the lift to come down?' Honey said.

'I might know what to do,' Fred said. 'We can fly up the stairs. Come on.'

Honey, Beanie and Hex all followed Fred up the winding staircase until they hit the top floor. They flew out of the stairwell through a window above the door and headed over to the lift. The garden was beautiful. It was a sunny morning and there were people digging in the vegetable patch, children playing and the woman with the glasses and the hat who they'd surprised before was sitting on a bench opposite the lift doors reading a newspaper.

'I think she's our best bet,' Fred said. 'She lives on the ground floor so she would have to take the lift all the way down.'

'How do you know where she lives?' Honey asked.

'She sometimes leaves blueberry muffins to cool on her windowsill. I know all the baked goods in this whole building.' Fred smiled. 'So, anyway, she's our best bet.'

'Best bet for what?' Hex asked.

'To get her to press the call button for the lift,' Fred said.

'So, are we just going to ask her? I could land on her paper and do a waggle dance to explain what we want,' Beanie offered.

'Somehow I don't think she  would understand a waggle dance, but I think that would be a good start anyway,' Fred said.

'What's your plan, Fred?' Honey asked.

'We basically have to annoy her so much that she gets up, gets in the lift and goes downstairs,' Fred said. 'As a fly I am particularly qualified to annoy humans. I pretty much do it all the time without even trying.'

'So, what do we need to do?' Hex asked.

'We buzz around her. Bump into the newspaper. Land on her hat and her glasses. Generally, just fly around and make noise. They hate that. Especially when they are trying to read,' Fred said.

'OK, let's do it,' Honey said. The four bugs all grouped together in a team huddle. 'Let's bug her for the bugs!' Honey shouted.

They flew over to the woman in the hat as she sat quietly reading.

First Fred dive-bombed her paper, pinging off it and startling her. She flapped the paper crossly and huffed. Then Hex and Beanie buzzed around her hat. She swatted them away with her hand.

'Watch out for the hands!' Fred warned. 'And if she rolls up the paper and starts swinging then we abandon the mission.' He shook his head. 'Rolled up newspapers are no joke to a flying bug.'

Then Honey went in and sat on the bit the woman was looking at on the newspaper. Every time the woman flicked the paper to get Honey to move, she would land back on the same paragraph so the woman couldn't finish what she was reading. The woman huffed again. She got up and moved to the other end of the bench.

'It's working,' Honey shouted. 'Just a bit more.'

They all dived in now and circled the woman's hat, buzzing as loudly as they could.

Finally, the woman slammed the paper down on the bench, folded it, tucked it under her arm and got up. She stormed over to the lift and pressed the call button.

Chapter 16

'Result!' Honey antennae high fived the others. 'We did it.'

The lift doors opened. The woman stepped inside. She pressed the ground floor button and opened up her paper to read again.

Very quietly Honey, Beanie, Hex and Fred slipped into the lift unnoticed and landed on a handrail. They tried not to make any buzzes to give themselves away.

The lift started to move. It travelled down, down, down. The ride would have been fine if it weren't for the small chocolate fingerprint that Fred spotted on the button panel of the lift.

'Chocolate,' Fred mumbled. 'It smells so lovely.'

'You can have plenty of chocolate later. I'm sure the guys in the balcony flat will bake something amazing this weekend but for now stay focussed, Fred,' Honey tried to calm him.

'I'll just have a taste. She won't even notice I'm there,' were the final words Fred said to the three young bees as he buzzed off towards the button panel.

He landed on the chocolate spot and did what flies do. They throw up a little bit on what they want to eat. It's gross to us (and to bees actually as well) but it's how flies digest their food. Fred smiled back at the young bees and started happily licking away at the chocolate spot he had just been sick on.

And, before you judge, remember this is totally normal fly snack behaviour.

'Did he just . . .?' Beanie started to say.

'Yup,' Honey answered. 'It's a fly thing.'

'At least he's quiet though,' Hex added. 'Maybe the woman won't notice.'

But the woman did notice. She saw Fred sitting there on the elevator button panel and then she did the one thing that all flying bugs fear more than any other. She rolled up her newspaper and took aim. As she raised her arm, poised to thump Fred with the paper, Honey, Beanie and Hex sprang into action.

'You're not thwacking our bug bro!' Honey shouted as they buzzed at the woman full on. Not stinging her but just buzzing around disorientating her so she couldn't hit Fred.

As the bees dive-bombed the woman, her rolled-up paper hit the buttons on the control panel: Blam! Blam! Blam! Blam! Meanwhile Fred flew out of the way of her weapon.

After what was only a few seconds but seemed like an endless journey to the four bugs, the lift landed with a gentle thud at the bottom floor. The sliding doors made their joyful *PING* as they slid open. The woman sighed and lowered the paper. She stepped towards the opening doors but suddenly let out a scream that definitely startled the ball of bees that was hovering outside the lift.

'AHHHHHHHHHHHHHHHHHHHHHHHH!'

she shouted. And raised the newspaper for battle again.

'Tell everyone to let her pass!' Honey said. 'And watch out for that newspaper!'

Bella shouted, 'You heard Honey, let the woman through.'

The ball of bees parted into two and the woman looked side to side like she couldn't believe her eyes. Then she ran screaming through the middle and out of the front door of the building.

'AHHHHHHHHHHHHHHHHHHHH!'

The doors pinged again.

'Quick – everybody in!' Honey shouted and the swarm of bees all zoomed into the lift just in time. The doors shut behind them and it started to move upwards.

Honey looked over and noticed that Her Majesty was looking distinctly nervous about this mode of travel. 'We have never travelled in a moving room before,' she said.

'It's a piece of cake,' Honey said.

'Cake?' Fred asked, looking around.

'Not literally cake,' Honey said. 'I mean it's easy. The room just goes up and down.'

'Unless it stops because someone has pressed too many buttons,' Fred said, and pointed to the control panel that had several buttons lit up.

Let's just say the trip took longer than expected.

I'll buzz you through the highlights.

The doors pinged open at floor three to a man with a very barky dog. The Queen was not amused.

The doors pinged open at floor seven and Fred had to be held back from flying out because he smelled a heavenly angel cake being baked.

The doors pinged open on floor ten to a baby in a pushchair who excitedly waved at the ball of bees and shouted 'Ball!' while her dad, who was looking at his phone, muttered, 'We'll play ball when we get outside.'

The doors pinged open on floor twelve to a very startled pizza delivery boy who just mumbled, 'I'll get the next lift. Go ahead.'

The doors finally opened on the roof garden and the people digging in the planters and the children that had been playing all stopped and stared as the ball of bees tumbled out into the fresh air.

The bees all spread out and explored the wonderful sights and smells of the bee paradise. They took in the scent of roses and jasmine and buzzed in and out of the trailing ivy leaves.

Honey wanted to show them why they'd come here though. The destination of their long journey. She needed to show them the abandoned hive.

Honey dashed over to it and all the other
bees followed.

She made a swooping loop-the-loop around
the top of the hive and shouted, 'TA-DA!!'

'Here it is. Our new home.'

Chapter 17

All the bees buzzed around the outside of the hive. And they all congratulated Honey on finding the hive. 'This is amazing, Honey!' 'I can't believe you found a new hive,' 'Wow! It's perfect here.'

'I didn't find it on my own. I had help from a certain flatfly I know.' She nudged Fred.

'Oh, that would be me.' Fred smiled.

'And my bee besties too.' Honey antennae high fived with Beanie and Hex.

The Queen hovered outside the entrance as well. Her eyes widened as she took in the sight. But her face fell a little too.

Honey whispered, 'I know it's not our old

home, but maybe we can make this one even better.'

'That is true. We must look on this as the opportunity it is,' the Queen said, smiling.

Miss Ivy peeked inside. 'It certainly is a . . .'

'Fixer-upper,' Fred offered.

'Yes, a fixer-upper,' Miss Ivy said.

'But there is so much potential,' Hex said. 'I need to get a team of builder bees together to work on how to make it work best for our needs, but this space will be great.' Hex immediately starting buzzing around the hive with a team of other builder bees.

'And we'll need to set up the nursery right away for all the new eggs Your Majesty will start laying soon,' Beanie said, following after Hex. 'Maybe start building the nursery first!'

The Queen smiled at Honey. 'Very well done, Honey. I look forward to having you as one of my companion bees, my dear.'

'Oh, I'm afraid that's no longer possible, Your Majesty,' Miss Ivy said. 'Honey and her friends will still have morning classes for Bee School, they still have some things to learn. Remind me to especially work on waggle dance practice this week.' She fluttered her wings.

'Then she can join me for her worker bee assignments in the afternoon,' the Queen suggested.

'Unfortunately not, Your Majesty. You see Honey now has a very different role in the hive.'

'What do you mean?' Honey asked.

'When a hive needs to swarm and move to a new hive, if they are lucky, a bee emerges who has the special skills to lead them to a new home. That bee is the scout bee. They are natural adventurers. And for the hive they can not only help to find a new home but find new sources of food, pollen and water.'

'That sounds like an important job,' Honey said.

'I think I know just the bee who could do it,' Bella said and ruffled Honey's stripy fuzz. 'Genius or trouble? There's a good chance you'll be both, but I wouldn't have you any other way.'

'So, I'm a scout bee now? I have a worker bee job? And it's ACTUALLY about adventure?' Honey asked.

'That's correct,' Miss Ivy said.

'And just to be clear, there is no larvae feeding involved, right?'

'Certainly not,' Miss Ivy nodded.

All the bees cheered and bounced Honey onto their shoulders.

'Oh, I nearly forgot,' she said. 'Can I take a very helpful flatfly along on my adventures?'

'Well . . .' Miss Ivy hesitated and looked over at the Queen, who shrugged and smiled. 'It's not how things are usually done but I suppose we might be doing things a bit differently in this new hive.'

'Indeed, we will,' the Queen said.

'Just one more question, Miss Ivy,' Honey asked. 'Do I have to start all this exploring right away or can I take a break?'

'I think you've all earned a break,' Miss Ivy said. 'But I thought you would be anxious to start your job filled with adventure.'

Honey said, 'I've had enough adventure in the last twenty-four hours to last me . . .'

Beanie interrupted: 'A lifetime?'

'Well, I was thinking for the next twenty-four hours,' Honey said. 'But what it has taught me is that Carl was right.'

'Who is Carl?' the Queen asked.

'He's a lone carpenter bee,' Honey said. 'He's very wise. I think I was jealous of his life on his own.' She looked at Bella. 'No one telling him what to do.' She looked at Miss Ivy. 'No rules. But Carl said I would miss a lot of my life here and he was right. He said there is a lot of good stuff in the Bee Code. Like about *"together, you see, you can be your best bee."* I spent so much time trying to do stuff on my own but it's when I was together with Fred, or Hex and Beanie, or Bella that I could really *"be my best bee"* and help the hive.'

'So, you don't want to be a human any more? Or a migrating bird? Or an acrobatic squirrel?' Bella asked.

'Are you kidding? Being a bee is the most exciting life ever,' Honey said, smiling at Hex and Beanie and then looking over at Fred and tapping his antennae. 'Especially if you get to hang out with a cool flatfly as a bonus.'

Bella smiled. 'Well, you guys can take a break, but we need to move the Queen into her new place, secure the area to make sure it's safe and get some food and water in for a pretty good moving-in hive party this afternoon. Lots to do.'

'Busy as a bee,' Miss Ivy said.

Honey, Beanie, Hex and Fred all lay down on the roof of the new hive while the buzz of setting up went on inside. They stared up at the sky and the floating clouds.

'Here's to lots more adventures,' Honey said.

'Yes, but maybe we could do that after dinner,' Fred said. 'Especially after dessert. I have to fly down to the balcony on the seventh floor and see what's there.'

Just then a voice came from overhead. 'Well, there's a surprise! Is that you, Honey?'

A beautiful butterfly fluttered overhead.

'Oh my buzzness! Bob, is that you?' Honey squealed and flew up to meet him.

Bob showed off his wings and his new look.

'You made a fab caterpillar, but you make an even more fabulous butterfly, Bob!' Honey said. 'This is Hex, Beanie and Fred.'

'Thanks, Honey. I was so worried about the change, but it's been brilliant. And I love the view from up here.'

'It's great, isn't it? And I know a bit about change after the day we've had. I feel like I transformed a bit myself. I'm a scout bee now.'

'Congratulations,' Bob said. 'Now, I'm a little hungry, I have a craving for something sweet. Do you have any suggestions around here?'

'Well . . .' Fred flew forward. 'Follow me to the best baking on the planet. Well, at least in the building. I thought I smelled angel cake . . .'

Fred, Hex and Beanie all led Bob over the edge of the roof and down to the balcony on the seventh floor. Honey looked out from the edge of the roof at her new home as the sun sat high in the sky and she wondered what adventures awaited her tomorrow.

Would there be travel, adventure, danger, mystery, flying battles with vicious wasps, or just more cake?

Hang on. That would be telling. You might just have to read the next book.

You wouldn't bee-lieve it!!!
Five Fun Facts about Bee-ing a Bee

Honeybees can touch, taste and smell with their antennae. They are super sensitive. They can even detect temperature and wind speed!

Bees use their wings not only to fly but to cool down the nectar as they make it into honey and to cool down the queen if she gets too hot. (Like bee power air conditioning.)

Honeybees have five eyes: three simple eyes and two compound eyes that are made up of many hexagonal facets. And their eyes are hairy! (Weird but true.)

Humans have kept honeybees for thousands of years. They were originally in baskets called 'skeps' and in large clay jars instead of the wooden hives that are mostly used today.

Bees don't only like flowers, they love flowering herbs as well. You could try planting herbs that bees like in your garden, window box or school garden. Chives, thyme, mint, rosemary, sage and basil are big bee favourites.